I'm Sorry

D0247066

BARTER BOOKS
ALNWICK STATION
NORTHUMBERLAND

For Dylan and Megan – J.E.

First published in hardback by HarperCollins*Publishers* Ltd in 2000
First published in paperback in Great Britain by Collins Picture Books in 2001

1 3 5 7 9 10 8 6 4 2

ISBN: 0 00 664629 8

Text copyright © Sam McBratney 2000
Illustrations copyright © Jennifer Eachus 2000
The author and illustrator assert the moral right to be identified as the author and illustrator
of the work. A CIP catalogue record for this title is available from the British Library.
All rights reserved. No part of this publication may be reproduced, stored in a retrieval system
or transmitted in any form or by any means, electronic, mechanical, photocopying, recording
or otherwise, without the prior permission of HarperCollins*Publishers* Ltd,
77-85 Fulham Palace Road, Hammersmith, London W6 8JB.

The HarperCollins website address is: www.**fire**and**water**.com

Printed in Hong Kong.

I'm Sorry

Sam McBratney

illustrated by Jennifer Eachus

Collins

An imprint of HarperCollinsPublishers

I have a friend I love the best.

I have a friend I love the best.

She plays at my house every day,
or else I play at hers.

I have a friend I love the best.
I think she's nice.

The things we do
always make me laugh,
and she thinks I'm nice, too.

She lets me be the teacher
when we teach our
toys to read...

...I let her be the doctor
and fix my bones.

We make her baby smile
when he wakes up
from his sleep...

...And sometimes we
put our wellies on

to see how deep
the puddles are.

I have a friend I love the best.
I think she's nice.

The things we do
always make me laugh,
and she thinks I'm nice, too.
But...

I SHOUTED at my friend today,

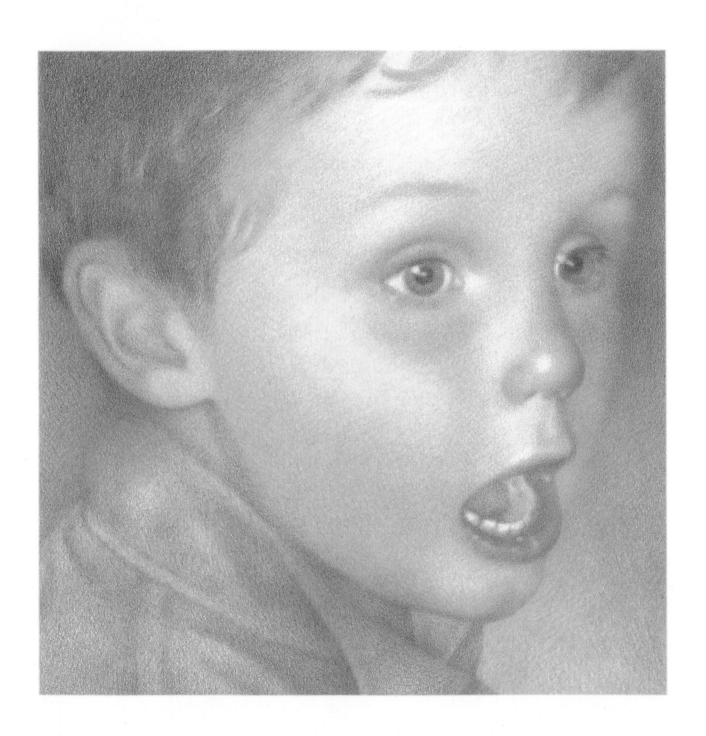

and she shouted back at me.

I wouldn't speak to
her any more, and
she won't speak to me.

My friend shouted at me today,
and I shouted back at her.
She wouldn't play with me any more,
and I won't play with her.

I pretend my friend's not there,

and she pretends she doesn't care, but...

I do care.

If my friend was as
sad as I am sad, this
is what she would do:

she would come and say, "I'm sorry,"

and I would say sorry, too.